Little Rabbit couldn't sleep

Albury Books

For Steph
B.S.

For Oliver and Joshua
S.A.

This edition published in 2020 in association with Crane Press

First published in 2009

Albury Books, Albury Court,
Albury, Thame, Oxfordshire,
OX9 2LP

www.AlburyBooks.com

978-1-910571-24-8

A CIP catalogue record for this book is available
from the British Library

Printed in China

Little Rabbit couldn't sleep

Albury Books

Little Rabbit
couldn't sleep...

In the day,
the sun is there,
warm and bright.

But when night comes,
the sky hangs low,
dark and empty.

"If I fall asleep now, there'll be no one watching over me," thought Little Rabbit. "I'll just have to wait for the moon."

And so he did just that.

The trouble with being
so tired and sleepy,
was that he didn't know exactly
when the moon would come.

Little Rabbit
waited and waited.

More time passed and the moon still hadn't come.

He thought he had better ask someone how much longer he might have to wait.

"This is my first day, ever,"
said a small flower in the fields.
"Maybe I will have grown into a tree
by the time your moon comes."

That sounded like an awfully long time.

Little Rabbit thought he had better
ask someone else – just to be sure.

"Look deep into the water," shimmered a little lake nearby. "Maybe your moon has fallen in and can't get out."

That didn't sound like what he wanted to hear.

Little Rabbit thought he had better ask someone else – just to be sure.

"Why don't you walk with me?"
   twisted a long and winding path.
"We can find out where I'm leading
   and maybe your moon is at the other end!"

That sounded like it might
be a long way away.

Little Rabbit thought he had better ask
someone else – just to be sure.

"I've just blown in to these parts,"
breezed a wind that had picked up.
"Who knows? I might be a big, fierce storm
by the time your moon comes."

That didn't sound like something
he wanted to wait for.

Little Rabbit thought he had better
ask someone else – just to be sure.

"We can't see your moon yet,"
rumbled the great, rolling hills.
"And we can see far into
the distance from up here!"

That didn't sound very promising.

Little Rabbit began to think
that the moon might never come.
And he was getting awfully tired...

And then, from behind the hills,
carried by the wind
along the twists of the path,
reflected in the lake,
and shining on the petals
of the small flower…

…the most perfect moon
slid into the night sky.

But Little Rabbit had fallen asleep, dreaming of the moon that would watch over him through the night.

For Steph
B.S.

For Oliver and Joshua
S.A.